# Who the [...] you, to put me in a zoo?

By Ben Lane

**Copyright 2019**
**See it for Real Publishing**
**First Edition**

**EPISODE 2**

**Sucker Punch**
A sucker punch is a punch that takes someone by
surprise. It is a punch that comes out of the blue.

EPISODE 1, Intermittent River is available on Amazon

"Freedom is not worth having if it does not include the freedom to make
mistakes" **Mahatma Gandhi**.

**Title song:**
Billie Eilish - *Six Feet Under*

**Other song suggestions:**
1. Aliotta Haynes Jeremiah - Lake Shore Drive
2. Sweet - Cigarettes After Sex
3. Xavier Rudd - Follow the Sun
4. Alice Phoebe Lou - The Tiger
5. Snow Patrol - Don't Give In
6. America - Horse with No Name
7. Still Corners - The Trip
8. Tracy Chapman - Fast car
9. Sigrid - Sucker Punch
10. Angus & Julia Stone - Heart Beats Slow

**Cast episode 2:**

1. William
2. Jo
3. Helen
4. Annabel
5. Mr Ramsbottom
6. Martin
7. Imogen
8. Lemmy (Tony)
9. Donald
10. Guy
11. La
12. Mr Wang

WILLIAM *is in a dentist room lying flat out on an*
*automated dentist chair. Mouth wide open.*

*He is squinting at a blinding light.*

*The hygienist, JO, is tackling WILLIAM'S teeth*
*furiously. Talking energetically as she does. WILLIAM*
*is massively hampered conversationally.*

*Between bouts of airy conversation, JO is measuring*
*WILLIAM's teeth. She mixes conversational pleasantry*
*and medical concern with considerable ease.*

*It's 10.22am. Overcast day.*

**CUT TO OPENING SCENE:**

JO: 4mm. Let me make a note before I forget. Ouch!

WILLIAM: *(Grunts).*

JO: 6mm. Dear me. That's not improving. You have a lot
of gunk in between the gaps. Tut. Tut.

WILLIAM: *(Grunts).*

JO: Have a rinse.

*The dentist chair moves into a sitting position very*
*slowly.*

WILLIAM *rinses his mouth out.*

WILLIAM: Am I in trouble?

JO: You have periodontal disease. Gum disease to put
it bluntly. And medically.

WILLIAM: Is that bad?

JO: We can't leave it like that. Back down. Expensive
work.

WILLIAM: *(Groans).*

*The dentist chair moves into the flat position very slowly.*

JO: 2mm. On the cusp. Busy day?

WILLIAM: *(Grunts and nods. The next words are barely audible).* School. Kids. Trouble at mill.

JO: School did you say? Or at the mill? I used to love school. 3mm. So, so.

WILLIAM: *(Grunts. The next words are barely audible).* Bloody. Kids. Ouch!

JO: Apologies. You've got kids? 2mm. Better. But still. Only average. Or rather, on the cusp. Is it one of those school meetings? The dreaded telling off type. 1mm. Super tooth.

WILLIAM: *(Grunts. The next words are barely audible).* Two. Boys. Idiots.

JO: I went through all that. My lot are fabulous people now.

WILLIAM: *(Grunts. The next words are barely audible).* Lucky. You.

JO: We are lucky. Blessed I would say. 5mm. One is a pilot. Well a glider pilot. I like gliders. Never been in one. But they look so peaceful. Graceful. 3mm. So, so. That's an ugly looking tooth.

WILLIAM: *(Grunts)* Thanks.

JO: There. We are done. Take off your bib and have a super big rinse. Sorry. Rinse first. Then bib off. I always get it the wrong way around. Arse about tit, me.

**CUT TO SUPERMARKET ON HIGH STREET:**

ANNABEL *is deeply lost in thought and placing what appears to be random items into her shopping basket. She approaches the checkout.*

*A tired-looking girl, HELEN, scans the items. HELEN begins to pack. HELEN realises her customer is deep in thought and possibly needs cheering up.*

HELEN: You okay?

ANNABEL: Sure.

HELEN: You look a bit lost.

ANNABEL: I'm fine. I've got some bags.

HELEN: 3 is it?

ANNABEL: 3. Yes. No 4. There is one inside this bag.

HELEN: 4 then. I have put that in for you. 4 bags. In total.

ANNABEL: Thank you. I'm fine. Really *(looking in her bags)*. Sorry. Oops. 5 bags. One was tucked inside the one tucked inside the other one.

HELEN: 5 it is.

ANNABEL: 5 bags. That should be it *(looks inside the other bags checking, lost in thought)*.

HELEN: Can I help any further? Shall I pack?

ANNABEL: Thank you. That would be kind.

*HELEN looks a bit put out that she has been asked to pack.*

**CUT TO OUTSIDE SCHOOL:**

WILLIAM *is hanging around outside a school looking awkward. A single, middle-aged man loitering around a school is not regarded well by the public. He checks his watch and looks frustrated. His mouth is still tender.*

*We see ANNABEL approach hurriedly. Flustered. Hot.*

WILLIAM: *(Pointedly at her)* Late.

ANNABEL: *(Pointedly at him)* Early.

**CUT TO INSIDE SCHOOL AND MR RAMSBOTTOM'S OFFICE:**

MR. RAMSBOTTOM *sits behind his desk.* ANNABEL *and* WILLIAM *enter and sit opposite him. No refreshments are offered.*

MR. RAMSBOTTOM: Here for an argument?

WILLIAM: *(Puzzled)* Certainly not. Is this where it's heading?

MR. RAMSBOTTOM: Good. Arguments next door. This room is for conciliation.

WILLIAM: *(Dawning on him)* And dead parrots I suppose?

MR. RAMSBOTTOM: Very good Mr, ummm *(studying his pad)*, Leith. Of course. Leith. Two Leiths in front of me. And two very naughty Leiths in the playground. Are you naughty Mr and Mrs Leith? Do you play in the playground?

*No answer from* WILLIAM *and* ANNABEL. *Just honest-to-goodness puzzlement.*

MR. RAMSBOTTOM: You spotted the Monty Python, ummm, reference I made. Big fan over here *(pointing to himself)*. Huge. Don't get me wrong. They were hit and miss. But their hits were simply glorious. Excellent news. How can we help? Do tell *(John Cleese in style)*.

WILLIAM: You asked us to come along. For a meeting.

MR. RAMSBOTTOM: Did I? I don't remember. Never mind. How can I help? F F F F Fire!

WILLIAM: *(Ignoring the oddness of* MR RAMSBOTTOM*)* We have a letter. Here.

MR. RAMSBOTTOM: Good news. May I see?

MR RAMSBOTTOM *takes the letter and reads.*

MR. RAMSBOTTOM: This is not good.

WILLIAM: No. It's not.

MR. RAMSBOTTOM: Are your kids okay? I mean in here *(taps the side of his head)*.

WILLIAM: I really don't know. Annabel?

ANNABEL: Of course they are. You stupid idiots. Can he say that? Can you say that Mr Ramsbottom? In a teacher capacity?

WILLIAM: *(To MR RAMSBOTTOM)* Of course they are okay in the head.

MR. RAMSBOTTOM: According to this letter, they are defi-nite-ly not. This is quite a list. Quite long. *(Reading from the list)* Theft. Bullying and theft. Bullying, theft and damage. Damage and theft. Bullying and damage. Theft, arson and bullying. Good god. Arson! I never knew. And so it goes on. *(More to himself)* Spam, eggs, chips and spam. Dear me, Leiths one and both. This is a list. Never in all my...

WILLIAM: Yes. Dear me. It's not good. It doesn't sound brilliant.

ANNABEL: Can you explain how the school has helped our boys. Guidance. Anything.

MR RAMSBOTTOM: We have tried all sorts. No more. Everything. No less. Conciliation. Appeasement. Kindness. Detention. Enforcement. Separation. Inclusion. We have got to the bottom of the list mam. No more things to go at. All the ions have been exhausted. No more ions in the fire. *(Short pause)* We have not, however, tried exclus - ion *(leaves the ion part of word hanging in the air)*. Nor indeed execution. Hanging and/or beheading.

WILLIAM: For both of them?

MR. RAMSBOTTOM: We won't hang and/or behead them. Not actually allowed. Silly banana.

WILLIAM: Exclusion I meant. For both of them?

MR. RAMSBOTTOM: Yes. Exclusion. Both. They are the Kray Twins of Manor Park School, Mr and Mrs Leith.

WILLIAM: Good god.

MR. RAMSBOTTOM: We found Bondi – our dear, sweet, kind Australian cousin - wrapped up in toilet paper on Tuesday. Top to toe. It had the hallmarks of the Leiths. And it wasn't a g'day for Bondi. I assure. Put him off his winter surfing classes.

WILLIAM: Good god.

ANNABEL: Was the toilet paper soft, strong and very, very Long.

WILLIAM: Christ. Get me outta here.

MR. RAMSBOTTOM: I think we have to decide about your boys. If I can be so bold, it may have to start at home. We can only do so much as a school.

ANNABEL: Only so much?

MR. RAMSBOTTOM: Only so much. May I ask? Do you like seafood? I know a great little fish restaurant. The three of us could... no?

*Nods of no from the Leiths.*

MR. RAMSBOTTOM: No interest? Shame.

**CUT TO PLAYGROUND:**

*We see the Leith boys,* TOM *and* TIM, *causing general chaos around the school. They are aged around 11 or 12. They are twins.*

*They obviously have a naughty streak. But they're no worse than any other kid who is grotesquely bored and simply wants to be stimulated by their school, the people around them. Not dragged down to the lowest common level of existence by society.*

**CUT TO INSIDE SCHOOL AND MR RAMSBOTTOM'S OFFICE:**

WILLIAM: They obviously have a naughty streak. We are aware. But they are no worse than any other kid who is grotesquely bored and simply wants to be stimulated by their school, their surroundings. Not dragged down to the lowest common level of existence by a 'we-are-all-equal' society shit. That is bollocks.

ANNABEL: *(Distractedly)* Nice. Very nice. I, on the other hand, think hanging and/or beheading is the only solution. Note the ion Mr Ramsbottom.

MR RAMSBOTTOM: Noted, Mrs Leith. Super, Mrs Leith. That is the only solute – ion *(the ion is emphasised)*. You sure about my fish supper idea?

ANNABEL: Thank you Mr Ramsbottom. We have children to chop up.

MR RAMSBOTTOM: I'll give them a week off school *(he stamps a piece paper with venom)*.

WILLIAM *and* ANNABEL *leave without further ado.*

**CUT TO HIGH STREET:**

*Same day. A little later on.* ANNABEL *and* WILLIAM *are walking together along the high street in discussion. They do not walk particularly near to each other.*

ANNABEL: Exclusion from school for a week is only fair. They are clearly disruptive little shits.

WILLIAM: They are 12 years old.

ANNABEL: Still. They need to grow up. And man up.

WILLIAM: They're 12 for god's sake. They are tiny little boys.

*We see* HELEN *(from the supermarket) further down the street arguing with a boy of her age. It looks very heated.*

ANNABEL: That's the girl from the checkout.

WILLIAM: *(Still focusing on his children)* It's strange. Their grades are above average. They're clearly not stupid. Demotivated perhaps. Defocussed. But not stupid. They are happy at home. Aren't they? Maybe we should do more with them?

ANNABEL: *(Not really listening, focussing on HELEN's argument)* That is one hell of a bust up.

WILLIAM: I could take them fishing.

ANNABEL: *(Distracted)* You should. *(Staring at HELEN)* Good god they are really going for it. I love a lover's tiff. So exciting. The pain for days to come. The delicious agony of it all.

WILLIAM: I'll get some bait. And hooks. Maybe beheading is the only solute - ion.

ANNABEL: *(Vaguely. More interested in watching Helen)* It is.

*We see the young lad HELEN has been arguing with storm off, jump in his van and drive away. Screeching his tyres in a manly fashion. HELEN looks at the boy's disappearing van with a mix of anger and sadness.*

ANNABEL: Is she alright?

WILLIAM: Who?

*Approaching HELEN.*

ANNABEL: Everything alright love?

WILLIAM *stands to one side awkwardly.*

HELEN: Oh it's you. Hello. The bag lady. Well he's a fucking fucker *(indicating the disappearing van with the angry boy inside roaring up the high street)*.

ANNABEL: Who is he?

HELEN: Only been shagging my best friend. Second time I've caught him. With his trousers down. Overall

shagging wanker. *(Shouting at the van)* filthy fuck
face.

WILLIAM: *(To* HELEN*)* Hi. I'm William. You know each
other? *(indicating* ANNABEL *and* HELEN*)*.

HELEN: The bag lady. Always got another bag inside a
bag. Yea. We know each other. Only for a few minutes.
She's always lost in her daydreams.

*We see the angry boy disappear in his van around a
corner. He sticks his hand out the window and gives a
middle-finger gesture. Then disappears for good.*

HELEN: Wanker!

ANNABEL: *(To* WILLIAM*)* You get back to work. I can
handle this.

WILLIAM: Right. Bye. Helen. Annabel.

*They both stare at him without an ounce of interest.*
WILLIAM *leaves them standing on the street.*

ANNABEL: *(To* HELEN*)* Shall we grab a coffee?

**CUT TO TUBE STATION:**

WILLIAM *is talking to a person in a ticket booth.*

WILLIAM: *(Midway through a conversation)* I have no
intention of getting a free ride. I have lost my
ticket.

MAN IN BOOTH: You need a ticket.

WILLIAM: Yes. Naturally. But I need a replacement. I
had one. But I lost it.

MAN IN BOOTH: You want a ticket?

WILLIAM: That is why I am here. For a ticket.

MAN IN BOOTH: For which zone?

WILLIAM: One.

MAN IN BOOTH: £2.80. Single.

WILLIAM: But I need a replacement. I had a ticket. But lost it.

MAN IN BOOTH: Yes. I know. £2.80.

WILLIAM: I'll walk.

WILLIAM *leaves the tube station and walks to the office.*

**CUT TO COFFEE SHOP:**

HELEN *and* ANNABEL *settle down with a coffee in a traditional café.*

ANNABEL: You okay?

HELEN: Had worse. *(Pause)* How does this go?

ANNABEL: How do you mean?

HELEN: Do you become my adopted mum for a day? Shall I kick off mummy? I didn't cry for the first 4 years of my life. I thought if I started, I wouldn't stop. Soon learnt that was dumb. I cry all the time now. And I like those moments when you do a thing and you're pretty sure no-one else in the world is doing the same thing. At that time. That's me.

ANNABEL: I'm an escort. £100 for 15 minutes. I won't wee on people. No weird shit. I sometimes give out freebies because I don't need the money. Although it all helps. By giving away a few free ones, it takes the seediness out. Makes it more respectable. I am in charge. Not them.

HELEN: There. Wasn't so hard. Now we can enjoy our coffee in peace.

**CUT TO OFFICE:**

WILLIAM *enters an open plan office on the third floor of a grey building.*

*It is dull and a little too quiet for comfort.*

WILLIAM *is not the boss. He is getting closer to the top job.* LEMMY *(an ex Motorhead fan) is the boss. He is clean shaven and does not have long hair. Or any bulbous facial markings. The name* LEMMY *stuck from what may be described as a wild teenage period. His real name is* TONY.

DONALD, GUY *and* SARAH *and others can be seen in the background.*

*Motivational* IMOGEN *is leaving* LEMMY's *office.*

IMOGEN: *(Behind her to* LEMMY*)* Next Tuesday then Lemmy. Module 4. It's a real Hellraiser. *(Spots* WILLIAM*).* Hi. William isn't it? The Rose call. *(Breezily)* I love that. You didn't make it easy. But it was fun to be part of. You never know what will happen. Yes?

WILLIAM: Yes.

IMOGEN: Can I use the Rose call in my training modules?

WILLIAM: Please do. I'm sorry about messing it up. Your seminar. Last week.

IMOGEN: Not at all. Bygones be bygones. *(Breezily)* Bye, bye gorgeous *(She gently touches his face).*

IMOGEN *leaves in flurry of red dress and red lipstick.*

WILLIAM: Goodbye.

*Imogen wiggles her hips ever so slightly.*

*Heart Beats Slow by Angus & Julia Stone plays.*

**CUT TO COFFEE SHOP:**

ANNABEL *and* HELEN *sit in silence sipping their coffee. It is drab outside. It seems all that needs to be said, has been said.*

**CUT TO OFFICE:**

WILLIAM *sits at his desk thinking. It seems all that needs to be said, has been said.*

**CUT TO OUTSIDE SCHOOL:**

TIM *and* TOM *create havoc.* BONDI *is hanging upside from a tree gently weeping. It seems all that needs to be said, has been said.*

**CUT TO INSIDE SCHOOL AND MR RAMSBOTTOM'S OFFICE:**

MR. RAMSBOTTOM *is playing table tennis using the wall of his office as his opponent. It seems all that needs to be said, has been said.*

**CUT TO COFFEE SHOP:**

*There is an almighty screech of tyres and a car crashes onto the pavement and through the café window where* ANNABEL *and* HELEN *sit in silence. The car ends up half inside the café. Glass, chairs, cups and tables fly everywhere.* ANNABEL *and* HELEN *scream and run to the back of the café. The dust settles. No-one is hurt. A man gets out of the car and stands among the settling debris and dust. It is* MARTIN. MARTIN *smiles beautifully through the dust. He is unhurt. He walks to the counter and grabs a bottle of water and downs it in one go. He loosens his tie.*

ANNABEL: Martin. It's you. You okay? Bloody hell.

MARTIN: Great. Never better. Hit a fucking pavement. Took flight. Airborne. Who's your friend?

ANNABEL: Helen meet Martin. My best client. My first client.

HELEN: What a fucking great entrance! I think I'm in love!

*All three stand and look at each other.* ANNABEL *frowning a little.* HELEN *and* MARTIN *smiling a lot. There is mild unease in the group dynamic.*

**CUT TO WILLIAM AND ANNABEL'S HOUSE:**

ANNABEL *and* LA *drink lakes of coffee and smoke copiously. The atmosphere is one of a party in full swing although the clock reads 10.22am.*

*A week has passed since* MARTIN *smashed through the window of the café.*

ANNABEL: I haven't seen him since. Helen is seeing him. Typical. He smashes up a café. Hurts no-one. And wins over a fragile but beautiful girl. A real Edie Sedgewick story. I miss him La. I miss our Tuesday togetherness.

LA: I miss him.

ANNABEL: Good god La. You haven't?

LA: I have. Twice. Both freebies.

ANNABEL: Well that's better. At least he pays me.

LA: Sometimes.

ANNABEL: What.

LA: Correction. He sometimes pays you.

*Short pause.*

LA: Fun, isn't he? Knowledgeable. But not cocky with it. Knows how it all works.

ANNABEL: Can we change the topic?

LA: How are the others?

ANNABEL *picks up her diary and reads out loud.*

ANNABEL: Getting busy. Full week. Mr A. That's Martin. No show this week. Damn his beautiful body. Shagging you. Not me. Mr B. Middle-aged. Kind. But clumsy. And very fast. Two-minute wonder. Mr C. Never again. Freak of nature. Mr D and Mrs D. New territory for me. Mr E is a new client. Arriving today. 3pm. A quick 15 minutes before the kids get home. A Mr Wang.

LA: Busy bee. The real Belle. How are the Kray Twins?

ANNABEL: Belle was a real person. Her name was Brooke Magnanti.

LA: Hark at you. You're all in the know.

ANNABEL: It wasn't easy having the boys off school last week and juggling this lot (*flaps her diary in the air*).

LA: (*Airily*) You've always been the world's greatest multitasker.

ANNABEL: I don't like call outs. Visiting people's homes. Way too much. So we find a park bench. Or a bush in a park.

LA: Get a room! How did you cope with Mr D and Mrs D on a park bench?

ANNABEL: We made do. In a bush. It was dangerous but extremely hot. You know. Bringing them both to climax in a public place.

LA: (*Dreamily*) I adore having you as my friend.

*It begins raining.*

**CUT TO WILLIAM'S OFFICE:**

WILLIAM *is at a meeting table with* DONALD, SARAH *and* GUY. WILLIAM is *seemingly in charge of proceedings.*

WILLIAM: Lemmy has asked me to arrange the company trip.

DONALD: Easy. Aviation museum.

WILLIAM: Maybe next year Donald.

GUY: Helping old people. In old people's homes.

WILLIAM: Some connection to our business would be ideal. However tenuous.

GUY: Helping bakers.

WILLIAM: That is our business.

DONALD: Helping bakers to fly?

WILLIAM: A bakers flying day out?

DONALD: Yes.

WILLIAM: Okay. That's decided. I'll go and tell Lemmy.

SARAH: *(Grinning)* Sounds fun. Will it be early to bed, early to rise?

WILLIAM: Doh!

GUY: Our very own Homer Simpson.

WILLIAM: *(Rises to go, resigned to his fate)* I'll go and tell Lemmy.

*The rest sit in silence looking uncomfortable.*

DONALD: *(Dawning finally)* Oh. I see. Doh! Dough. Bread. Clever. Really good.

GUY: And the early to rise bit. Get it? They are all bread puns.

SARAH: You two are totally great. You know that.

**CUT TO LEMMY'S OFFICE:**

WILLIAM *sits opposite* LEMMY. *He has clearly explained the idea for this year's company trip.*

LEMMY: Bakers flying. How does that actually work?

WILLIAM: I am thinking we arrange a bake off at the aviation museum and the winner gets to fly in a jet plane. Eating their winning baked item in mid-air. Be great for marketing. You Tubers will love it. Good for local awareness. Eating a baked item at Mach 1. Upside down. Nothing beats that.

LEMMY: I love it. The Flying Bakers! Sponsored by Bradshaw the Bakers. 123 years of baking tradition. 37 shops nationwide. Always rising to the challenge.

WILLIAM: 38.

LEMMY: Hmmm.

WILLIAM: 38. Letchworth opened last month.

LEMMY: 38 is it? Well blow me down.

WILLIAM *leaves* LEMMY's *office and sits down at his own desk and puts his head in his hands.*

WILLIAM *appears to drift into a peaceful slumber.*

WILLIAM *enters a dream sequence. He is at an airport with a hammer and he begins to smash his way through an airplane cockpit door. A man dressed as a tiger approaches and asks: Who the fuck are you? WILLIAM replies that he is not sure, but he has an airplane to break through and for the tiger to please leave him in peace. The tiger ignores him, picks up a hammer and starts to help WILLIAM smash through the airplane cockpit door and says: We can do it William. We can do it. Don't Give in.*

*Don't Give In by Snow Patrol plays.*

SARAH: William. What did he say? Wakey, wakey.

WILLIAM: *(Still half asleep)* I need to get on the plane.

SARAH: Wake up. What did Lemmy say?

WILLIAM: *(Shaking himself awake)* He loves it. The Flying Bakers. Planes and bread. Mach 1. Upside down. Eating cake.

SARAH: Sounds fun. Donald will be in heaven.

WILLIAM: It's the yeast I could do. The yeast? Doesn't work so well. Never mind.

**CUT TO WILLIAM AND ANNABEL'S HOUSE:**

ANNABEL *sits on her own in the kitchen. The clock reads 2.57pm.*

MR WANG *is due anytime for his 15 minutes with* ANNABEL.

*There is a knock at the door. We see* ANNABEL *rise and walk to the door. She opens it to reveal* MR WANG.

ANNABEL: Mr Wang.

MR WANG: How do you do.

ANNABEL: I'm fine.

MR WANG: Annabel. Beautiful. Sexy lady.

ANNABEL: *(Eying him up happily)* Thank you. You little charmer.

MR WANG: 15 minutes will be plenty of time.

ANNABEL: No rush Mr Wang.

*Grizzly Bear by Angus & Julia Stone plays softly.*

MR WANG *steps into the house and stands in the hall looking confident. Removes his wallet. He hands* ANNABEL *a pile of notes.*

*They mount the stairs.* ANNABEL *is leading the way and guides* MR WANG *very, very gently.*

**CUT TO MARTIN'S HOUSE:**

HELEN *and* MARTIN *are in bed. It is the afternoon. They both look very relaxed.*

HELEN: Let's get away from here.

MARTIN: Where?

HELEN: Anywhere hot.

MARTIN: ~~Okay.~~

HELEN: I love you.

MARTIN: I love you. How about South America?

HELEN: Where is that?

MARTIN: Near North America.

HELEN: You always make things so clear. I love that about you. And this *(her hand creeps under the duvet).*

**CUT TO WILLIAM'S OFFICE:**

WILLIAM *calls across the office.*

WILLIAM: It's on folks. The Flying Bakers sponsored by Bradshaw the Bakers.

DONALD: Fan - fucking - tastic. I just love this place. Flying jet planes!

DONALD *waltzes across the office making airplane noises.*

WILLIAM: Right, I'm going home. Early for once.

**CUT TO SUPERMARKET ON THE HIGH STREET:**

*A little later we see* HELEN *and* MARTIN *at the supermarket where* HELEN *works.*

*They are both prowling the aisles and occasionally putting items in their jacket pockets. They walk out the exit looking a bit bulgy.*

HELEN *(To her boss on the way out)* See you tomorrow. Bright and early!

*They run off giggling.* HELEN's *boss waves them off smiling inanely, muttering to herself: 'young people. So much fun being young!'*

**CUT TO WILLIAM AND ANNABEL'S HOUSE:**

ANNABEL *and* MR WANG *descend the stairs. There is a knock at the door.* ANNABEL, *in a panic, pushes* MR WANG *into the living room.*

ANNABEL: *(whispering)* Hide, hide. Fuck, fuck.

MR WANG: *(Jokingly)* Fuck, fuck.

ANNABEL: Fuck off. In there. Keep down.

ANNABEL *pushes* MR WANG *really hard into the living room and we hear him topple over. And grunt painfully.*

ANNABEL: *(Dramatic whisper)* Now shut the fuck up.

ANNABEL *composes herself and opens the door.*

MARTIN *is standing on the threshold with a bunch of flowers. And a big white smile.*

MARTIN: I'm back.

ANNABEL: You are. Like the Terminator. I'm back.

MARTIN: Can I come in?

ANNABEL: No. You can't. I have someone here. In there *(points to the living toom)*.

MARTIN: Bad timing.

ANNABEL: Very bad.

MR WANG *pokes his head out of the living room.* MARTIN *sees him.* MARTIN'S *face changes to a look of thunder.*

MR WANG: *(Not noticing MARTIN)* Can I come out please?

ANNABEL: No. Fuck off back in there.

MARTIN: Him! Mr Wang!

ANNABEL: You know Mr Wang?

MARTIN: (*To* MR WANG) Mr Wang.

~~MR Wang: Hello Mr Smith.~~

ANNABEL: You know each other? This is Mr Wang.

MARTIN *flies at* MR WANG *and knocks him flat with a sucker punch: a punch that comes from out of the blue. MR WANG collapses to the floor and falls into the living room. For a second time.*

MR WANG *is out for the count.* MR WANG *can't be seen from the front door.*

WILLIAM *appears at the front door. He sees* MARTIN's *back in the door frame and* ANNABEL *facing him in the hallway.*

ANNABEL: (*Looking around* MARTIN) William. You're home. (*To* MARTIN. *Slight pause*). I am. We are. We are not interested in any double glazing. Single glazing. Any bloody glazing. Get it. Now leave me - us - alone. Go!

MARTIN *skulks off. He does not look at* WILLIAM.

WILLIAM: We need a sign on the door. No cold calling. This street is not what it was. Thought I would surprise you. Donald was driving me insane.

ANNABEL: (*Undecided*) Brilliant! Come in. I mean. Let's go upstairs. Right now. It's been too long. Lots of lovely sex. Now.

WILLIAM: I bet you say that to all the boys.

ANNABEL *pushes* WILLIAM *up the stairs. They mount the stairs.* ANNABEL *is behind and pushes* WILLIAM *very, very roughly and quickly up the stairs.*

MR WANG *is still in a comatose state in the living room. Blissfully unaware.*

WILLIAM: God. You're keen.

ANNABEL: Get upstairs big boy.

**CUT TO OUTSIDE SCHOOL:**

TIM *and* TOM *are sitting with* BONDI *on a school bench. They share sweets with* BONDI. *All seems well in their relationship.* BONDI *laughs at their jokes. He is enjoying their company.*

MR RAMSBOTTOM *walks by and notices this new-found happy relationship with some satisfaction.*

MR RAMSBOTTOM: *(To himself)* Lovely to see.

**CUT TO WILLIAM AND ANNABEL'S HOUSE:**

*It is obvious some time has passed.* WILLIAM *descends the stairs. He has wet hair and is wearing a dressing gown. He walks into the living room. He comes back out shortly after.*

WILLIAM: *(Calmly calling upstairs)* Darling. Why is there a Chinese man asleep in the living room?

ANNABEL: *(From upstairs)* Fuck! Fuck!

WILLIAM: Again?

ANNABEL *descends the stairs also with wet hair and wearing a dressing gown.*

ANNABEL: A what!

WILLIAM: In there. A Chinese man. Fast asleep. Hardly a whimper.

MR WANG *begins to come around. He stumbles to his feet. He rushes out of the living room, pushing* WILLIAM *roughly to the floor. He crashes through the front door and runs down the street.*

ANNABEL: Who the hell was that!

WILLIAM: *(His nose bleeding)* You don't know?

ANNABEL: Absolutely no idea. It's like a zoo around here. Double glazing salesmen. Chinese people.

WILLIAM: Animals. All of them.

ANNABEL: Just what the hell is going on?

WILLIAM: This neighbourhood is on the downward turn.
That seems quite definite.

ANNABEL: You're bleeding darling.

WILLIAM: Superficial wound. That was fantastic
*(glancing upstairs)*. You've got some new moves. Some
great shakes. I'm loving it. Reminds me of the
Antarctic. Do you forgive me for that disaster?

ANNABEL: Let's book a holiday. Just the two of us. The
Antarctic could be fun. Get some perspective back.

WILLIAM: About time we did something for us.

ANNABEL: Yes. Just for us. Get away from this.

WILLIAM: A fleeting moment of freedom. I like it.

**CUT TO THE RECYCLING CENTRE:**

*We see WILLIAM wearing a pair of boxing gloves and
walking to skip 9 at the recycling centre. A burly man
who works at the tip approaches WILLIAM and tells him
that he is about to use the wrong skip. He needs skip
12 for boxing gloves. Not skip 9.*

WILLIAM *raises his gloves in a mock boxing stance. He
has no intention of starting a fight. He's just
playing around. The burly man thinks otherwise and
knocks WILLIAM to the ground with one swift punch.*

WILLIAM *lies among the debris of the recycling centre,
out cold. He is wearing boxing gloves and his arms are
splayed out. WILLIAM's tooth rolls along the ground.*

*Sucker Punch by Sigrid plays out.*

**Fade
Credits**

**Other ramblings by the same author**

**Dying on Air**

A 10-minute play about a host and radio guest picking through their lives on air.

**Michelin Stars**

A dark comedic play about fine dining, treachery, love and a great deal of Béchamel sauce.

**In Three**

A play consisting of three interconnecting parts exploring various moments of love, laughter and life.

**The List**

A play over the course of one day consisting of dark comedic moments and horrific murders. Set in a small English town.

**The author**

https://seeitforrealpublishing.wordpress.com/
Facebook: @seeitforreal

Printed in Great Britain
by Amazon